Dear Vincent

I hope you enjoy my book.

Love,

Sudy Palmer

The Little Bird of Many Colors

Gula H. Palmer

Illustrated by Joshua and Raina Chelise

ISBN Number: 978-0-69201931-3

Professional Press
Chapel Hill, NC 27515-4371

Manufactured in the United States of America

12 13 14 15 16   10 9 8 7 6 5 4 3 2 1

Dedication

I would like to dedicate this book
to my five children and seven grandchildren,
especially the youngest, Shayne.

This story is about a Mother Bird and her baby bird, who live on Mr. Brown's Farm. Mr. Brown has a large farm, with many animals, crops and trees. It is in one of these trees, our story takes place.

High up in one of farmer Brown's trees, sat a lovely brown bird with a pretty red breast, and she was called a Robin. The mother Robin had been in her nest, lying on her only egg, waiting for her baby bird to hatch. She was so excited to see her first born, and to see if the baby would look exactly like her. She would leave her nest and go into the corn fields and oat fields, looking for nice, large worms to feed her baby bird when it was born.

The day finally came when the baby bird popped out of the tiny egg. Mother Bird picked up her baby and held it in her wings and fed it lots of food, and decided to name him Little Bird. After several days, the feathers of the little bird started growing and to the mother's surprise, they were all different colors. The little bird looked something like a rainbow. At first, the Mother Bird was scared, but then the more she thought about it, the happier she became. Just think, her baby would be one of a kind—now wouldn't that be special!

Mother Bird was teaching Little Bird how to fly one day, when a worker from the farm took a look at them and shouted out; "Wow, what a sight! I just saw a very funny looking bird of many colors." This made Mother Bird very angry to think that someone would make fun of her beautiful baby. When something is different, people can be very mean.

The days went by and one morning when the Mother Bird was looking for food, one of her wings got caught on a branch and bent it. Mother Bird fell to the ground and could not fly anymore. After a long time, Farmer Brown who was working his crops, spotted Mother Bird on the ground. He picked her up and took her to his house, where he placed her in a cage and told her he would heal her wing so she could fly again. Mother Bird was very sad and wondered what would happen to Little Bird, if she did not come home.

Back in the nest, Little Bird of Many Colors wondered where his mother was, as he was getting very hungry. He decided to drop out of the nest, but found that he could fly, so he would now look for his own food.

Little Bird's first encounter was a large, funny animal, and he didn't know at the time, it was a beaver. The beaver said, "Hello there. You certainly are a different looking bird, but very pretty. Can I help you in any way?" Little Bird began telling him about his Mother and asked Beaver if he could help him across the stream, as he couldn't quite fly very far. Beaver said, "Sure, hop on my back and I'll swim you across." When they reached the other side, Little Bird thanked Beaver for his kindness and thought to himself, "Boy, I have already made one new friend, and my Mother would be proud of me."

Now on this side of the stream, Little Bird felt hungry so went in search of food. He found some nice leaves to rest on while he filled his stomach with some big worms, and that made him feel really good. It was getting late in the day and soon night would arrive, so since he did not have a nice warm nest to lie in, he thought he'd find somewhere warm to sleep and then search some more tomorrow.

The next day Little Bird began his search and came upon some sheep grazing in the field. Little Bird thought that their wool coats would be warm and a nice place to sleep. A large sheep suddenly talked to Little Bird, telling him, "Get away from me you funny looking bird!" This really hurt Little Bird's feelings, so he moved away.

Then out in the field he saw a different colored sheep among the rest of the white sheep, and it was black. Little Bird went up to the black sheep and said, "I am looking for my Mother and I need a warm and safe place to sleep tonight, so I can search more tomorrow. Black Sheep said, "Sure, because you are different like me, that makes you special, so hop on!"

Little Bird was so happy to have a warm place that night and a nice friend. The next morning when Little Bird woke up, as he was leaving, he thanked Black Sheep kindly and thought to himself, I have already made two new friends and I think I am really special and that makes me happy.

On the second day of Little Bird's search, he came upon another different looking animal, with a black and white fluffy tail. While Little Bird watched this animal he noticed that other creatures around him kept far away. Little Bird decided it was because this animal looked different like him, so he decided to ask him if he had seen his Mother.

As Little Bird began to tell his story, the skunk smiled and said, "Why Little Bird, you are so brave to come up behind me and talk to me. When I am surprised, I make a stinky smell to keep others away from me, but you are different like me, and I am very happy to have someone to talk to. I will walk with you in the woods today to look for your Mother and find food. Then you can stay with me in my den tonight to stay warm." It was so much fun, thought Little Bird, being with Mr. Skunk all day. They laughed and played and found lots of good things to eat. "I am so happy," thought Little Bird, "to have made another friend and my Mother would be very proud of me. Even if you are different, you can still be OK in every way." On the morning of the third day, Little Bird said goodbye to Mr. Skunk and thanked him for his kindness, so off he went to find his Mother.

19

Back at Farmer Brown's house, Mother Bird stayed at the farm until her wing had healed. Farmer Brown was getting ready to release Mother Bird, so she could fly back to her nest. She was so happy, that before flying away, she flew back to Farmer Brown, landed on his hand and made a big chirp, as a thank you. Farmer Brown said, "Go on your way now and good luck," and gave her a big wave as she flew away.

Little Bird was learning to fly pretty well, so it made his search a little easier. As he was sitting high in a tree while taking a rest, he spotted something really exciting. It was a large bird that he had never seen before, flying so fast, up and down, from the sky to the ground. Wow, he thought, "If I could fly like that bird, then I could really find my Mother much faster." Little Bird thought that he would call out to that fast flying bird and ask for his help.

Little Bird called out, "Hello, can you help me?" Within seconds, that big bird was by his side. The big bird said, "I am a hawk and there are many animals and people who do not like me or are afraid of me, but I am here for a special purpose, the same as you are." Little Bird was so happy that he began telling Mr. Hawk about his search for his Mother. Mr. Hawk continued, "Since I am so fast and know the forest very well, I can help you find your Mother, so climb on my back."

They searched the forest for a long time and then Little Bird remembered that he had crossed the stream with Mr. Beaver. Little Bird said, "Mr. Beaver took me across the stream, so please cross me back over the stream." Mr. Hawk flew back across the stream and within a few moments they saw a nest, and just below it on a branch sat Little Bird's Mother. Oh, what a wonderful surprise for everyone!

Mother Bird thanked Mr. Hawk for returning Little Bird home. She should have been afraid of Mr. Hawk, because hawks can be dangerous, but on this special day, with this special Little Bird, they were ALL FRIENDS.

So if you ever happen to see this Little Bird of many colors, say "hi" for me.

THE END